Flash the Fish

Written by
Alison Maloney

Illustrated by
Maddy McClellan

meadowside BOOKS

Flash the Fish
splished and splashed
in the pretty paved pond.

Dig the Dog licked and picked at a big, **beefy** bone.

Gill the Gull
spied and eyed
the pretty paved pond.

Flash the **Fish** darted and dived in the deep, **dark** depths.

Gill the Gull
flapped and flew
from the ruby red roof.

then swooped and scooped,
Flash the **Fish** out of the
clean, **cool** pool.

Dig the Dog started and darted towards **Gill the Gull.**

Kit the Cat jumped and bumped into Dig the Dog.

Flash the Fish wiggled and wriggled.

Gill the Gull spluttered and fluttered towards the sizzling, summer sun.

Dig the Dog and Kit the Cat raced and chased the big, bad bird.

Gill the Gull
cawed and soared
over the ruby red roof...

...and landed on the **boggy** brown bank.

Kit the Cat
crept and leapt
at Gill the Gull.

Dig the Dog
prowled and howled
behind Gill the Gull.

Gill the Gull stopped and dropped Flash the Fish into the rushing, **gushing** river.

Flash the Fish swirled and swept towards the **fierce**, flowing falls.

Kit the Cat slipped and slid into the rushing, gushing river and whirled and twirled towards the fierce, flowing falls.

Dig the Dog looked and leapt
in the deep, dark depths
then clamoured and clung
to a big, broad branch.

Kit the Cat grappled and grabbed
Dig the Dog's fat, fluffy tail.

Flash the Fish
swung and hung on
Kit the Cat's
sleek, silky tail.

Dig the Dog
scrabbled and scrambled
onto the **boggy** brown bank
then hauled and **heaved**
Kit the Cat.

Dig the Dog
stopped and popped
Flash the Fish
into his moist mouth...

...and leapt over the **great**, garden gate, then stopped and dropped **Flash** the **Fish** into the pretty paved pond.

Gill the Gull squawked and stalked the long, lush lawn.

Kit the Cat and **Dig the Dog** blinked and winked...

...then **shook** and showered Gill the Gull!

Flash the Fish
flapped and clapped
while Kit the Cat
and Dig the Dog
cheered and
jeered!

For Tamsin and Spencer,
Two very special people
A.M.

For Rafael and Inigo
M.M.

First published in 2009
by Meadowside Children's Books
185 Fleet Street London EC4A 2HS
www.meadowsidebooks.com

Text © Alison Maloney 2009
Illustrations © Maddy McClellan 2009
The rights of Alison Maloney and Maddy McClellan
to be identified as the author and illustrator
have been asserted by them in accordance with
the Copyright, Designs and Patents Act. 1988

A CIP catalogue record for this book is
available from the British Library

10 9 8 7 6 5 4 3 2 1
Printed in Indonesia